Dave Saunders trained at Brighton Art College.
He worked as a primary school teacher for many years
and is now a full-time author/illustrator of children's books.
Together with his wife, Julie Saunders, who is a librarian,
he has created several young picture books for Frances Lincoln
including *The Ducks' Winter Tale*, *The Brave Hare* and *The Big Storm*.
He has also illustrated *Down by the Pond* by Margrit Cruickshank.
Dave and Julie live in Malvern Link, Worcestershire.

For Tom

The Ducks' Tale
Text copyright © Julie Saunders and Tony Bradman 1990
Illustrations copyright © Dave Saunders 1990

First published in Great Britain in 1990 by
Frances Lincoln Limited, 4 Torriano Mews
Torriano Avenue, London NW5 2RZ

First paperback edition 1990

British Library Cataloguing in Publication Data
available on request

ISBN 0-7112-0607-4 hardback
ISBN 0-7112-0608-2 paperback

Set in Century Schoolbook

Printed in Hong Kong

5 7 9 8 6 4

THE DUCKS' TALE

Dave and Julie Saunders

FRANCES LINCOLN

It was a lovely summer's day. Dibble and Dabble, the two white ducks, were swimming in the river.

Suddenly in the reeds they saw something very strange.
It was a furry snake!
Dibble and Dabble were scared. They jumped into the
water and swam up the river as fast as they could.

Under the bank they met Vole.

"What's the matter?" said Vole.

"We've seen a long furry snake in the reeds,

and we think he's coming!"

"Wait for me," called Vole.

Beside the lilypads they met Frog.

"What's going on?" said Frog.

"We've seen a scary long furry snake in the reeds,
and he's coming this way!"

"Wait for me," croaked Frog.

In the shady glade they met Fish.

"What's up?" said Fish.

"We've seen a horrible scary long furry snake

in the reeds, *and he's coming after us!*"

"Wait for me," said Fish.

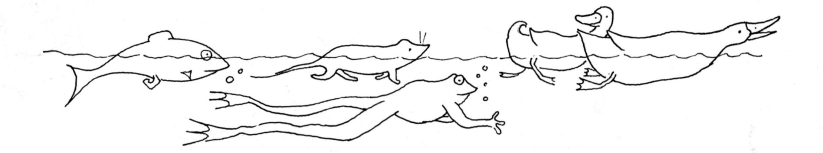

By the old tree stump they met Kingfisher.

"What's the rush?" said Kingfisher.

"We've seen a fat horrible scary long furry snake

in the reeds, *and he's coming closer!*"

"Wait for me," said Kingfisher.

In the shallow bay they met Heron.

"Where are you all going?" said Heron.

"We've seen an enormous fat horrible scary long furry snake in the reeds, *and he's close behind us!*"

"Wait for me," said Heron.

They met Pete in his boat.

"Steady on you lot," said Pete. "What's the matter?"

"We've seen a gigantic enormous fat horrible scary long furry snake in the reeds, *and he's chasing us!*"

"Follow me," said Pete. "We'll go and see."

Back downstream they all went, back to the reeds.

Pete stopped the boat and everyone gazed.

The furry snake moved and. . .

began to disappear and. . .

turned into Tigger the cat.

How they all laughed!

MORE PICTURE BOOKS IN PAPERBACK FROM FRANCES LINCOLN

THE BIG STORM

Dave and Julie Saunders

Dark clouds are gathering over the wood. "Hide and shelter!" cry the animals one by one, running into their holes and burrows. As the storm breaks, the Squirrels find an unlikely hiding-place and, when the rain stops, a surprise treasure-trove as well!

Suitable for National Curriculum English - Reading, Key Stage 1
Scottish Guidelines English Language - Reading, Levels A and B
ISBN 0-7112-0865-4 £3.99

THE BRAVE HARE

Dave and Julie Saunders

Hare is hungry, and tells all his farmyard friends of his plan to feast among the cabbages.
"Oh no. You can't do that!" they cry, and one by one they warn him of the terrible things he will find there.
But tales of furious farmers, giants and monsters don't deter the brave Hare in the slightest -
and he proves his well-meaning friends wrong...

Suitable for National Curriculum English - Reading, Key Stage 1
Scottish Guidelines English Language - Reading, Levels A and B
ISBN 0-7112-0761-5 £3.99

RED FOX ON THE MOVE

Hannah Giffard

When a bulldozer tears apart the den of Red Fox and his family, they find themselves on the move.
In their search for a new home, they encounter an angry snake and an owl. Finally, after taking refuge
on a barge, they wake up in the city, where they find their perfect hole in a beautiful wild garden.

"Hannah Giffard is an original, the undiscovered talent publishers dream about." The Bookseller

Suitable for National Curriculum English - Reading, Key Stage 1
Scottish Guidelines English Language - Reading, Levels A and B
ISBN 0-7112-0819-0 £3.99

Frances Lincoln titles are available from all good bookshops.

Prices are correct at time of publication, but may be subject to change.